Actually, I Used to Be a Princess

Third printing by Willowisp Press 1997.

Published by Willowisp Press
801 94th Avenue North, St. Petersburg, Florida 33702

Cover design © 1997 by Willowisp Press

Printed in the United States of America

4   6   8   10   9   7   5   3

I S B N   0 - 8 7 4 0 6 - 8 4 4 - 4

Actually, I Used to Be a Princess

story & pictures
by Unada

I haven't always lived here.

Actually, I used to be a princess.

When I was a princess, I lived in a castle with seven tall towers.

But one day when I was sailing my boat on
the moat, I was stolen away by bandits.

The king was simply furious.

"When I catch those kidnappers I'll toss them in a dungeon and throw away the key!" he yelled.

Everyone in the country went looking for me.

The bandits got scared.

They decided to dump me on a doorstep.

This family took me in.

They're really very nice people.

But back in the days when I was a princess,
I always ate from a golden plate.

And I never had to set the table.

People paid attention to me when I was a princess.

Now nobody listens.

Some people even think that they know more than I do.

When I was a princess, I had people like that put in the dungeon.

Of course, when everyone was in the
dungeon, sometimes I did get a little lonely.

At least I don't get lonely around here.

But when I was a princess I had my very own room. And there was no little sister around to mess it up, either.

I had a whole tower full of toys when I was a
princess. And I never had to share.

Well, sometimes sisters share.

I was a very important person when I was a princess. I always appeared with the king and the queen at parades and fairs and market openings.

But that was really just about the only time
I ever saw the king and queen. They were
very, very busy.

I see quite a lot of this family. They're around more than the king and queen ever were.

NOT AGAIN!

And, of course, when I was a princess I didn't get out of the castle very often. There were giants hiding in the woods outside. At least once a month there was a dragon smoking and snorting at the castle gate. It was safer inside.

Now that I live here I get out a lot more to
do things with friends.

Sometimes it's even nice to share a room.

It's great to be a princess, but
when I think about it . . .

. . . I really like being here.